THE VIDEO GAME BANDIT

HARDY BOYS

→ Clue Book ← #1

THE VIDEO GAME BANDIT

BY FRANKLIN W. DIXON ← → ILLUSTRATED BY MATT DAVID

ALADDIN

NEW YORK   LONDON   TORONTO   SYDNEY   NEW DELHI

ALADDIN

An imprint of Simon & Schuster Children's Publishing Division
1230 Avenue of the Americas, New York, NY 10020
This Aladdin paperback edition April 2016
Text copyright © 2016 by Simon & Schuster, Inc.
Illustrations copyright © 2016 by Matt David
Also available in an Aladdin hardcover edition.
All rights reserved, including the right of reproduction in whole or in part in any form.
ALADDIN is a trademark of Simon & Schuster, Inc., and related logo is
a registered trademark of Simon & Schuster, Inc.
THE HARDY BOYS and colophons are registered trademarks of Simon & Schuster, Inc.
HARDY BOYS CLUE BOOK and colophons are trademarks of Simon & Schuster, Inc.
For information about special discounts for bulk purchases, please contact
Simon & Schuster Special Sales at 1-866-506-1949 or business@simonandschuster.com.
The Simon & Schuster Speakers Bureau can bring authors to your live event.
For more information or to book an event contact the Simon & Schuster Speakers Bureau
at 1-866-248-3049 or visit our website at www.simonspeakers.com.
Book designed by Karina Granda
The text of this book was set in Adobe Garamond Pro.
Manufactured in the United States of America 0518 OFF
6 8 10 9 7 5
Library of Congress Control Number 2015933127
ISBN 978-1-4814-5053-9 (hc)
ISBN 978-1-4814-5052-2 (pbk)
ISBN 978-1-4814-5054-6 (eBook)

CONTENTS

THE VIDEO GAME BANDIT

A PARTY FOR CHAMPIONS

"This way, over here!" Frank Hardy called out. He waved his arms back and forth, signaling his younger brother, Joe. Joe walked across the backyard with a stack of folding chairs. They were kind of heavy, and his face was beet red after carrying them over to Frank and their friend Ellie Freeman.

Frank and Joe's baseball team, the Bayport Bandits, was having a big fund-raiser. They were hoping to go to Florida on a team trip and play a few friendly games with other teams. In between games the team would be at the beach, snorkeling, paddleboarding, and learning how to surf.

Ellie's parents had volunteered to host the fundraiser at their house. They had a big backyard, where they would auction off prizes in honor of the Bayport baseball team. People from all over town had donated things for the auction—a meal at Chez Jean, the fanciest French restaurant in Bayport, sailing lessons, art classes, and a shopping spree at Blair's Boutique, a cute new store in town.

"What do you need next?" Joe asked Ellie. He dropped the metal chairs on the ground with a clatter.

"I think we need to get the tablecloths from my mom," Ellie said. She was busy unfolding another stack of chairs and setting them up in a straight line. The stage in the backyard was already assembled, and now they were figuring out where the guests would sit during the auction. A big van from Forks and Knives was parked near the side door of Ellie's house, and the workers were busy shuttling delicious-looking food from the van into the house. "This party is going to be the best in Bayport history," Frank said, looking at the decorations they'd just hung up. There were lights and streamers strung across the yard. "Do you think we'll raise enough to go to Florida?"

"You bet." Ellie grinned. "The tickets alone will give our fund a huge boost. Then we have the prizes that will be auctioned off and the fashion show—all the boutiques donated clothing just to be part of it."

"Sounds like we'll be in Florida in no time," Joe laughed. He unfolded a chair and set it down next to one of Ellie's.

With twenty-five kids on the team, it would be expensive to fly everyone down and have them stay at a hotel. They'd already had a bake sale and a car wash. With this huge event, everyone was hoping they would raise all the money they needed to bring every member of the team to Florida for free—or at least to pay for everyone's plane ticket.

As Frank and Joe helped Ellie set up the rest of

the chairs, Mrs. Freeman came out, followed by Phil Cohen, a friend from school. He was carrying a small speaker that he put down by the side of the stage. "You guys remember my friend Biff, right?" Phil asked. He pointed over his shoulder.

A tall blond boy came out of the house with the other speaker. He was wearing a blue T-shirt with the word TIGERS written across it in orange script. Right behind him was a basset hound puppy with long, floppy ears, who scampered down the stairs, tail wagging.

"Hey, guys!" Biff called. "Long time no see!"

Before Frank or Joe could even respond, the puppy jumped up on them. Frank crouched down as the puppy covered his face with wet kisses.

Biff ran over, grabbing the back of the puppy's collar. "Come on, Sherlock! Down!" he commanded.

"Sorry, he's still learning," Biff apologized.

"That's okay," Frank said, rubbing the puppy's head. "He's great."

"Sherlock?" Ellie asked, kneeling beside them. She kissed the puppy on the nose. "That's so cute."

Phil looked at his friend. "Biff and Sherlock are staying with me for the weekend while Biff's parents are away. He's helping me set up the music for the fund-raiser this afternoon," he said. "I figured we could use an extra hand."

"Isn't that nice of him?" Mrs. Freeman said as she darted past. She put a stack of tablecloths on one of the tables. "It's true, we could use all the help we can get."

"I just hope this guy doesn't cause too much trouble," Biff said, rubbing Sherlock's head. He looked down at the dog. "You're going to be a good boy, aren't you, Sherlock? Aren't you?"

"Let's hope!" Mrs. Freeman said.

Sherlock sprinted across the lawn, his ears flying up behind him. He grabbed a branch that had fallen from a nearby tree and started chewing it. As

Frank and Joe helped Ellie with the tablecloths, Phil and Biff went to work on the sound system. Frank looked over at Biff, trying to remember the last time he'd seen him. Phil had been friends with him for a long time, but Biff didn't go to the same school as they did. Frank and Joe usually only hung out with him at Phil's birthday parties every year.

Just then Mr. Freeman came around the side of the house. Mr. Fun, the owner of the local arcade, was right behind him. "Look who I found outside!" Mr. Freeman said. "Mr. Fun came to drop off his prizes for the auction."

All of them stopped what they were doing when they saw what Mr. Fun had brought. "Is that what I think it is?" Phil Cohen asked excitedly. He studied the box in Mr. Fun's hand. He was holding a ZCross5000, a video game system that had just come out the month before. *Every* kid at Bayport Elementary wanted one.

"The ZCross5000!" Mr. Fun said. "You bet it is! I waited in line at the store for five hours the day it came out. Then I came home, only to find out

Mrs. Fun had already gotten me one for my birthday. Figured you guys could use the extra for the auction. Oh . . . and these!" He held up some free passes to Fun World, his arcade.

Frank and Joe grinned. Mr. Fun had given them a whole stack once, after they'd solved a mystery at the arcade. They were known around Bayport for helping people find missing pets, stolen bikes, or even jewelry. Just a month before, they'd helped figure out who had played a prank on their good friend Chet Morton.

"This is going to be the highlight of the auction!" Mr. Freeman exclaimed. "I heard every store is sold out of the ZCross5000 now."

"They are!" Mr. Fun said. "I hope this helps the team get to Florida."

Mrs. Freeman and Ellie had climbed onto the stage. They unrolled a large banner that said THANK YOU FOR SUPPORTING THE BAYPORT BANDITS! The

Freemans had put large wooden posts in the ground, and Mrs. Freeman and Ellie hung the banner in between the posts. Ellie took a few steps back, trying to get it in just the right spot. "How does it look?" she finally asked.

"Perfect," Joe said. They all stood there, staring at the backyard. All the chairs were set up in rows now. With the decorations they had already put up, the backyard was looking great. Mrs. Freeman had even put floating candles in the pool, which looked pretty fancy.

"This is going to be so much fun," Mrs. Freeman said as she taped the banner in place. "And with a little luck, we'll have enough in the fund to send all of you to Florida for lots of baseball and sunshine!"

Frank wrapped an arm around his brother. "Soon we'll be at the beach, catching some waves!"

"Or snorkeling," Ellie chimed in.

"Or playing beach volleyball," Joe added.

Frank smiled. "Or—"

"Let's not get excited just yet!" Mr. Freeman said.

He waved for them to go back inside. "There's still work to do. We have to set up all the trays for appetizers. We need to organize the buffet table. And you three need to change into your Bayport Bandits shirts before the guests get here."

He pointed to Frank, Joe, and Ellie. They headed inside, Phil, Biff, and Sherlock following behind them.

Frank leaned toward his brother. "Not get excited?" he whispered. "That's impossible!"

Chapter 2

LET THE BIDDING START!

"Would you like to try a coconut shrimp?" Joe held the silver tray high in the air. A woman with stiff white hair picked up a shrimp and put it on her plate. Onstage, the fashion show was in full swing. Cissy Zermeño stood in the center and did a twirl. She wore a pink dress with a wide-brimmed white hat.

"Thank you so much, Cissy!" Mrs. Freeman announced. She stood at the edge of the stage, reading from a stack of note cards. "Again, her outfit was from Lulu's Corner."

Just then their gym teacher, Mrs. Kingsman, walked across the stage in a green plaid suit. "Mrs. Kingsman is wearing a crisp Weathersby suit from Blair's Boutique," Mrs. Freeman announced. "The jacket is cropped at the waist and has tortoiseshell buttons. She's wearing it with a white ruffled blouse. Perfect for work or a business dinner. Doesn't she look sharp!"

The crowd applauded as Mrs. Kingsman strode down the steps and into the house. The fashion show had been going on for about half an hour. Miss Swivel, who worked in the Bayport Elementary School's cafeteria, modeled a long blue parka. Everyone laughed when their art teacher, Mr. Hendricks, came onstage wearing a bright orange sweater and furry hat.

"And now for our last model before we start the auction," Mrs. Freeman said. "Give a round of applause for . . . Principal Green!"

The crowd cheered as Principal Green stepped onto the stage. Most of the Bayport Bandits were weaving in and out of the audience in their baseball T-shirts, passing out appetizers. Ellie, Joe, and Frank put their trays down on a nearby table to clap for their principal. She was one of the Bayport Bandits' biggest fans.

Principal Green spun around in the center of the stage and smiled. Her dark hair was curled like she was going to a fancy ball. "Principal Green is wearing a purple polka-dot skirt with a gray silk blouse from Blair's Boutique. Doesn't she look lovely!"

Principal Green waved to the Bandits before she headed off the stage. As the audience watched the show, Frank and Joe walked through the crowd, picking up crumpled napkins and empty plates. Ellie passed out a tray of tiny hot dogs, giving a few extra to Sherlock. The puppy was wandering around the lawn, a Bandits bandanna tied around his neck. Every now and then he'd stop to beg for food or tear apart one of the paper plates that had fallen on the ground.

Phil pressed a few buttons on the sound system, and music filled the air. There were a ton of people in Ellie's backyard. Some were sitting at tables, eating the last of their food. Others sipped their drinks and talked about the fashion show. Everyone seemed excited that they could find the outfits in local stores.

Ellie found Joe as he was giving away the last of his shrimp. "Can you believe it?" she asked. "The party is a total success so far!"

"Everyone seems really happy to be here," Joe agreed.

"I just heard a group by the pool talking about the auction. One man wants to bid on the ZCross5000 for his grandson. He doesn't care how much it costs," Ellie added with a huge smile.

"Get your paddles ready!" Joe said, pretending he was the announcer. "The bidding starts in five minutes!"

Ellie and Joe were raising their hands, pretending to bid on different items, when Frank waved to them from across the lawn. "Guys! Over here!" He pointed at the photo booth set up by Ellie's old swing set. Mr. and Mrs. Freeman had hired someone to take pictures of all the guests.

Ellie and Joe crammed inside with Frank as the flash went off. It went off again and again. Ellie, Joe, and Frank made funny faces for the camera, wearing some of the props in the booth. There was a crown, a big pair of glasses, and all kinds of unique hats. They were having so much fun, they hardly noticed when the music stopped and Coach Quinn came onstage to start the auction.

"The first prize up for auction is a cooking lesson with Chef Jolene, of Jolene's Bistro!" she called out. "The bidding starts at fifty dollars."

A woman with red hair raised her paddle, which meant she wanted the lesson. But almost as soon as she did that, another woman raised her paddle. That meant the price would be higher because she wanted the lesson too. The women kept bidding against each other until the red-haired woman won.

"Going once . . . going twice . . . sold for eighty

dollars!" Coach Quinn called out. Cissy—or Speedy, as most people called her—was the pitcher for the Bandits. Everyone called her Speedy because she did everything super-fast, from talking to pitching her famous fastball! She had changed out of her fashion show outfit and was now in charge of bringing out the prizes. When she came onto the stage with a certificate for the cooking class, everyone cheered.

Frank and Joe sat by the pool as Coach Quinn auctioned off the other prizes. There were sailing lessons, art classes, and a gift certificate for a month's worth of free ice cream from the new ice cream shop in town, Two Spoons. Mrs. Zermeño, Cissy's mom, ended up bidding on a spa weekend. Mr. Carson, the woodshop teacher, had donated a hand-carved chair that went for a lot of money.

"Sold to the man in the gray hat!" Coach Quinn called out. Cissy moved the wooden chair to the right of the stage and put a red tag on it that said SOLD. Then she disappeared inside, looking for the next prize.

Coach Quinn smiled at the audience. "Thank you so much for your support today. You've all been so generous with this auction. Now I'd like to announce the last prize up for bidding. Everyone in town has been talking about the ZCross5000, the new gaming system from MegaKidz. But not many people have been playing it—the gaming system has been sold out for over a month, and it's hard to find. Today we're putting one up for auction, thanks to Mr. Fun from Fun World."

The crowd clapped. A few boys in the front row stuck their fingers in their mouths and whistled loudly. "Yeah! The ZCross5000 rocks!" one yelled.

Coach Quinn looked toward the house, waiting for Cissy to come out with the prize. A minute passed, then another. She made a few jokes to keep the audience's attention, but that only worked for so long.

"Cissy?" Coach Quinn said into the microphone. "Are you there? Will you bring out our next prize? The ZCross5000?"

Just then Cissy appeared at the back door. Her cheeks were bright red, and she looked like she might cry. Mrs. Freeman ran to her, trying to figure out what was going on. "Cissy, what is it?" Mrs. Freeman asked. "What's wrong?"

Cissy crossed her arms over her chest. "The ZCross5000 . . . Someone took it. It's gone!"

A SINGLE CLUE

"This has to be a mistake," Mrs. Freeman exclaimed. "Who would steal something from us? Who would do that?"

She looked back at the crowd, noticing that everyone was still watching Cissy and her. A few women in the front row were whispering to one another. An older man with white hair looked shocked.

Coach Quinn grabbed the microphone. "If you could excuse us, we'll need to put the auction on hold while we figure this out. In the meantime, please enjoy the dessert table!" She pointed to the other side of the patio, where a table with cookies and cakes was set up. Slowly everyone got out of their seats. Some people were still looking at Cissy and wondering what had happened.

"Do you really think someone took it?" Joe said, turning to his brother.

"I don't know," Frank replied. "Let's go see."

Cissy and Mrs. Freeman had already disappeared inside the house. Frank and Joe found them in the den. Mr. Fun was there too, along with Mr. Freeman.

"It was right here," Cissy repeated. She pointed to a spot on the floor. "I left it with some of the other prizes."

Frank and Joe scanned the den. There was a long couch, a coffee table, and a television set. In one corner was Ellie's piano, and in another was a polka-dot beanbag chair. A few family photos were on display, but other than that, the walls were bare.

"Oh, good." Mr. Fun turned around, noticing for

the first time that Frank and Joe had come inside. "You're here! What do the two best detectives in Bayport think?"

Joe was about to respond, but then he noticed Frank. His brother was on the other side of the coffee table. He knelt down and picked up a few sheets of paper. "Instructions for the ZCross5000," he whispered.

Joe walked over to get a better look. The paper booklet was ripped down the center. It looked crumpled around the edges, too. "Maybe whoever took the ZCross dropped this on their way out," Joe said.

"They were probably in a hurry," Frank added. "They definitely opened the box."

"There aren't any other signs of it, though," Joe pointed out.

"Could this be a mistake?" Mrs. Freeman asked. She kept

rubbing her temples with her fingers. "Maybe someone accidentally took it."

"I don't think so. It had a sign on it that said 'For the Auction.'" Cissy shook her head. "I saw it about half an hour ago. A few of the bigger prizes were in here, but most of the other stuff was in the dining room. I don't know what happened."

"I can't believe this," Mr. Fun said. "Whoever is responsible must be caught. They can't just walk away with it! It's maddening!"

"We'll figure out who did this," Frank promised. He scanned the room again, checking to see if there was anything they might have missed.

"I hope so," Mrs. Freeman said. She glanced out the window, where the party was still going on. "The auction was supposed to be over around five o'clock, but I don't know how long people will stay if we can't even find the biggest auction prize."

Joe pulled his notebook from his back pocket and flipped to a clean page. "There's no time to waste, then," he said. "Let's get started."

Chapter 4

THE FIVE *WS*

Joe wrote *The Five Ws* at the top of the page and underlined it twice. Whenever they were trying to solve a mystery, they started with a few simple questions. He wrote *Who?*, *What?*, *Where?*, *When?*, and *Why?* underneath the heading.

"Let's start with a possible motive," Frank said. "Why would someone want to take the ZCross5000?"

Mr. Fun laughed out loud. "Well, that's easy!

Because it's a ZCross5000! Who *wouldn't* want to take it?"

THE 5 Ws
Who?
What?
Where?
When?
Why?

"I'm afraid Mr. Fun is right," Mrs. Freeman said. "Everyone in Bayport—not to mention the whole country—wants one."

Frank walked the length of the room. "Because it's expensive and they could sell it. Because they wanted one for themselves. Because they couldn't get it anywhere else. Those are three possible motives."

Joe wrote all three down. Frank and Joe's dad, Fenton Hardy, was a private investigator. He'd taught them all about motive, which was just another way of saying why someone would do something. Every crime had to have a motive, and sometimes the motive helped you find the suspect.

"How many guests are at the party?" Joe asked.

"About a hundred," Mrs. Freeman answered. She sat down on the couch and crossed her arms over her chest. "I'm so upset. What a horrible ending to the afternoon."

"It's not over yet. Is there anyone here that you think might do something like this?" Joe asked.

Mrs. Freeman shook her head.

Suddenly Mr. Fun snapped his fingers. "Wait, I remember—I did see someone."

Joe put his pen to the paper, ready to copy down everything Mr. Fun said.

"At the beginning of the party," Mr. Fun went on, "there was a girl hanging around the den and the dining room, by the prizes. She kept looking into the other rooms, like she was searching for something. She seemed really suspicious."

Frank glanced at his brother. Most of the guests had spent the afternoon outside. It was strange that the girl had been in the house, and even stranger that she was exploring all the rooms. "Do you remember what she looked like?"

"She had a purple shirt with polka dots on and a pink streak in her hair. Her hair was brown. I think. I'm not sure."

Joe scribbled some notes. He wrote *Pink streak in hair, purple shirt with polka dots*, then a few notes

about where she'd been in the house. "Is there any one else who might have done it? Anyone else you can think of?"

Mr. Freeman pointed to the closed door on the other side of the room. He lowered his voice when he spoke. "The kitchen is right there. Do you think one of the workers from Forks and Knives might have taken it?"

"I don't think so, Ed," Mrs. Freeman said. "They

wouldn't. Besides, we've had them work for us at other parties. Why would they suddenly start stealing things now?"

Mr. Freeman nodded. "You have a point, but there were two or three people working in the kitchen today. Even if one of them didn't take it . . . maybe they saw something strange. If anyone used the kitchen door that goes outside, the workers would've noticed, right?"

Mrs. Freeman looked like she might argue with him, so Frank jumped in. "We'll question them just in case. It helps to have witnesses, too."

Joe looked at Cissy. "You said that you saw the ZCross here just half an hour ago?" he asked.

Cissy looked uncertain. "I think it was half an hour ago, but then again . . . I'm not sure. I thought I saw it at the beginning of the auction, whenever that was."

"I think the auction started right at three o'clock," Mrs. Freeman added. She pointed to Joe's notebook, as if to say, *You should probably write that down.*

"So the ZCross could've disappeared anywhere between three o'clock and now—four fifteen." Frank plopped down in the beanbag chair, deep in thought.

Joe wrote down *Between 3:00 p.m. and 4:15 p.m.* under *When?* He wrote *ZCross5000* under *What?* That was always the easiest question to answer. *Where?* was simple too. The ZCross had been taken from the Freemans' den, where it was waiting to be auctioned off.

"I really don't think the workers had anything to do with it," Mrs. Freeman repeated.

"Don't worry," Joe said, looking at the list. "We'll figure out what happened. We should start by talking to the girl Mr. Fun mentioned."

Frank stood and peered out the back window and into the yard. There were a bunch of people around the side of the stage, looking at the prizes from the auction. Guests were still using the photo booth. Some were huddled around the dessert table, piling cookies onto their plates. It was a huge crowd of people, and Frank didn't see a girl in a purple shirt anywhere.

"We just have to find her," he said. "And we don't have much time."

Joe joined him, scanning the crowd. "Agreed. But where should we start?"

Chapter 5

PICTURE PERFECT

Joe squeezed through the crowd, moving around toward the pool. There was a group of kids he didn't recognize. He thought they might've been some of Ellie's friends from camp. He looked at each of the girls' outfits, but none of them matched the description Mr. Fun had given.

"Have you seen a girl with a purple shirt and a streak in her hair?" Joe asked a blond boy with glasses.

The boy just shrugged. "A streak? What do you mean?"

"Her hair was colored—she had pink in it," Joe explained.

The boy shook his head. A few of the other girls were playing tag on the lawn. They stopped for a moment, watching Joe. "I think I saw someone like that, but I don't know her name," a girl with braces said.

"Do you remember where?" Joe asked.

"No, just that she was here at the party somewhere," the girl explained. "Sorry."

Joe had wasted almost twenty minutes walking around in circles, trying to find the girl Mr. Fun had mentioned. He was starting to wonder if she actually existed. He'd checked all the rooms in the house, making sure she wasn't hiding somewhere. He'd looked at the tables by the pool and studied the groups of people sitting on the chairs by the stage. He'd even gone to the edge of the woods behind the backyard, where Ellie's old playhouse was.

He spotted Frank across the lawn, by the dessert

table. "Did you find anything?" Frank called out.

"Nothing," Joe said. He walked over and picked up a chocolate chip cookie. "Maybe she already left."

"Look," Frank said, pointing to the photo booth across the way. "Are you thinking what I'm thinking?"

"It couldn't hurt to check," Joe said. "There's a chance she might've taken a picture there. We might find some more clues."

The boys took off across the lawn, waiting in line while Cissy's parents posed in front of a background with the Bayport Bandits logo. "Looking good!" the man behind the camera said. "Let's see your big smiles!"

Mrs. Zermeño held a feathered fan and wore a floppy hat with ribbons on it, and Mr. Zermeño had goofy sunglasses on. They both looked nervous. They straightened up as soon as they saw Frank and Joe. "Did you find anything? What happened?" Mrs. Zermeño asked, turning to the boys.

"Nothing yet," Frank said.

Joe went over to the man behind the camera. He was a tall, skinny guy with suspenders and a fedora. He had his laptop computer on the table in front of him. With a few clicks of the mouse, he printed out copies of the pictures of Mr. and Mrs. Zermeño. They didn't look very happy in any of the pictures.

"Let us know if we can help with anything. This is just terrible," Mrs. Zermeño said, before walking off.

"You want to take another turn in the booth?" the guy asked. "I'll be closing it up in a little bit."

"Actually, we were hoping you could help us with something," Frank explained. "Do you keep all the pictures on your computer?"

"Yeah," the guy said. "Just about. Unless someone really hates the photo and wants me to delete it. But eventually they all go up on the website the day after the party."

Joe glanced sideways at his brother, knowing they were onto something. "Can we see them? We're looking for a girl who had a pink streak in her hair. We were hoping she stopped by here."

"That sounds familiar," the guy said. He clicked through screen after screen of photos. Finally he stopped on a set of four. Sure enough, they were pictures of a girl in a purple shirt with brown hair. One piece in the front was dyed pink.

"That's definitely her—she matches the description," Joe added.

The guy hit print, and a strip of four photos came out. "Here, so you have it."

Joe and Frank studied the pictures. In them, the girl in the purple shirt was next to a girl with short blond hair. Freckles covered her nose and cheeks. She looked a year or two younger than the girl with the short hair—maybe she was eight or nine. They were making angry punk-rock faces in two of the photos, and silly faces in the others.

"Thanks for this," Frank said. "Now we have something to show people."

"I don't think I saw either of them," Joe whispered as they scanned the crowd.

"Me neither," Frank added. They pushed past a group of teachers who were talking about the fashion show. Principal Green was in the center of them, making a joke about the furry orange hat Mr. Hendricks had to wear.

The boys checked the backyard again. They checked the patio and the playhouse. It wasn't until they went back to the dessert table that they spotted her. The freckle-faced girl was there alone, taking a bite of chocolate cake.

"Can we talk to you?" Joe asked, walking up to her. "We were hoping you could tell us who your friend is."

The girl's green eyes widened. "Where'd you get those?" she asked, looking at the strip of pictures. "Those are mine."

Before Joe could answer, she plucked the photos from his hand. "We've been looking for your friend," he said.

"Why?" the girl asked. "We aren't friends. Where'd you find these?"

"The guy from the picture booth gave them to us," Frank explained. "What do you mean, you aren't friends?"

"Never mind," the girl with freckles said. Frank was about to ask her more, but the girl turned on her heel and headed across the lawn, to where the other kids were playing tag.

"That was really weird," Joe whispered.

"Really weird," Frank agreed. "Why would they take pictures together if they aren't friends?"

As they stood there, watching her join the game of tag, they were more confused than ever.

"She's hiding something," Joe finally said. "The only question is what."

Chapter 6

A SECRET IN THE WOODS

Frank and Joe were still standing there, confused, when a little boy with red hair and freckles came up to them. He had chocolate around his mouth. He couldn't have been more than six or seven years old.

"Do you guys know my sister, Lisi?" he said. He pointed to the girl with the freckles. She was running across the grass, reaching out to tag a boy with curly black hair.

"Kind of," Frank said. It wasn't a lie . . . not really.

"Have you met her friend with the pink streak in her hair?" Joe asked.

"Kendall," the little boy said. "But Mom and Dad said they weren't allowed to hang out anymore. They always get in trouble when they're together."

Joe raised his eyebrows at his brother. No wonder Lisi had been so nervous when she saw the pictures of them together. She probably hadn't realized they would be on the website, or that anyone else would see them. If she wasn't allowed to hang out with Kendall, the pictures might get her in trouble.

"Do you know where we could find Kendall?" Frank asked.

The little boy shrugged. "I don't know . . . she was here before. My mom says Kendall likes doing her own thing. What does that mean?"

Joe scratched his head. It might have seemed like a small detail, but it would definitely help them. He and Frank had spent the last half hour looking in all the most crowded places. Maybe they should have been looking in the quiet rooms of the house, or the places no one else would go.

"I have an idea," Joe said, waving for Frank to follow him. They thanked the boy as they headed off to the back of the yard, where the woods began.

"Where are we going?" Frank asked.

"To the quietest place there is," Joe said. "Ellie's old tree house. I walked around it before, but I never looked inside."

"Good thinking," Frank said. He followed Joe, his feet crunching down on dry leaves and twigs. Soon they could see the tree house through the trees. It was dirty, and all the shutters were closed.

When they got there, Joe knocked on the tiny door. "Kendall? Are you there?"

One of the shutters opened, and the girl with the pink streak in her hair peered out. "Who's asking?"

"We just have a few questions for

you," Frank said. "Someone saw you in the Freemans' house around the time the ZCross went missing. Did you see anything strange?"

"Ugh," Kendall sighed. She closed the shutter and opened the door, letting them in. Frank and Joe both had to duck a little to walk around. They noticed she had a sketchbook. She was drawing different objects in the house—an old plastic teapot and some broken crayons.

"I hope you didn't tell my mom I'm back here," she huffed.

"No," Joe said. "We don't even know who your mom is."

"We did talk to Lisi," Frank said. "Are you two friends?"

Kendall laughed. "Yeah, just don't tell her parents that. That's why I was in Ellie's house before. Lisi and I had a plan to hang out during the fashion show, when her mom wouldn't notice. She's still upset over this expensive vase we broke the last time I went over to their house. It was a total accident! I tripped and fell!"

"So you were in the house during the fashion show? Where?" Joe asked.

"We actually stayed on the front porch, playing Spit. You know that card game?" Kendall said.

"Who won?" Frank asked.

"Lisi did—she's pretty good." Kendall sat down on the floor of the playhouse and crossed her legs. She closed her sketchbook and put it in her lap.

"Did you see anything suspicious?" Joe said.

"Nope. You can ask Lisi, too, if you want—she was with me the whole time." Kendall twisted the piece of pink hair around her finger. "Is that it? I want to finish my drawing before the party ends."

Joe looked at his older brother, wondering if they were thinking the same thing. Kendall seemed to be telling the truth. She hadn't even paused when Frank asked her who won the card game.

"I think that's it," Frank said.

"Let us know if you remember anything else," Joe added before they left.

When they were far enough away from the

⌐ 39

playhouse, Frank finally spoke. "I think she's telling the truth," he said.

"Me too," Joe agreed. "Which means our only other lead is the workers Mr. Freeman mentioned."

Frank sped up, walking faster back to the party. "Let's talk to them as soon as we can," he said. "Everyone will be leaving soon—we're running out of time."

Chapter 7

TOO MANY COOKS

As Joe and Frank made their way back to the house, they noticed the party was quieter than before. A lot of guests had left. Phil had abandoned the stereo, putting on music that sounded like what you'd hear in an elevator.

"Mrs. Freeman seemed pretty sure the people who helped set up the party didn't have anything to do with it," Joe said. "If they've worked at other parties at Ellie's house, it doesn't make sense that they'd suddenly walk in and take the ZCross. What would be the point of that?"

"It's our only lead now," Frank said. "We have to follow it."

Their dad had taught them about leads, which were clues that pointed the investigator in a certain direction. This one was leading them to the people who worked for Forks and Knives. There was a reason Mr. Freeman had mentioned them, and they had to explore it. As they walked into the kitchen, they tried to stay hopeful. Maybe Mr. Freeman was right. Maybe the workers *did* know something about the missing ZCross.

A man with a white bandanna around his head was washing dishes. A few other people brought trays in from outside. Frank, Joe, and the rest of the Bandits had met all the workers at the beginning of the party. For most of the event the Bandits had been going inside and picking up appetizers, then passing them out to all the guests.

A blond woman was arranging a plate of giant brownies. She looked up when Frank and Joe walked in. "Can I help you?" she asked.

"We were hoping to talk to you about the missing video game system—the ZCross everyone's been looking for."

The woman sprinkled some powdered sugar on the brownies. "Wish I knew more, but I didn't see anything. What about you, Larry?"

The man with the bandanna shrugged. "Nothing."

Joe pulled out his notepad, hoping a few questions might help them remember something. "Did you notice anyone go into the den from the kitchen? Or maybe they came out of the den? We think whoever took it would have left this way—otherwise they would have had to go through the backyard."

The woman had a white jacket that said HEATHER on the front in curly script. She pulled a lemon custard pie from the fridge. "I didn't, but I was busy prepping the desserts."

Just then a teenage girl came into the room. She looked like she went to Bayport High School. She had her hair in a ponytail and was wearing a shirt that said FORKS AND KNIVES. She put a pile of dirty dishes into the sink and turned to go.

"Excuse us!" Joe called out. "Did you see any-thing strange this afternoon? We're trying to figure out who took the ZCross from the den. We still haven't been able to find it."

The girl threw up her hands. "I just told Christina, but she didn't think it meant anything!" She laughed.

Heather and the man with the bandanna both turned, suddenly interested. "What do you mean?" Joe asked.

"I saw two kids right before the auction. They came out of the den. They both had something under their shirts. They were practically running out the front door." The girl put her hands on her hips.

Joe started writing down everything she said. "What did they look like?"

She shook her head. "I didn't get a good look, that's the problem. They were moving too fast. But the one kid . . . whatever he was holding under his shirt . . . it looked like it was alive."

"What?" Frank said loudly. "What do you mean?"

"It was squirming," the girl said.

"A boy with a squirming stomach? This is starting to sound like an alien movie." Joe laughed. He wrote it all down anyway.

"I think the other kid had the game. There were, like . . . cords and stuff coming out from under his shirt. It wasn't in the box anymore." The girl shrugged. "I don't know what else to tell you."

A boy with glasses and braces came in with another tray of dirty dishes. He set them down on the counter. It was obvious that he'd been listening to their conversation. "I saw those kids too!" he cried. Frank noticed that his name tag said KEVIN. "You're right, Alana. I was taking some dishes out to the van and saw them come out too. I heard them talking about some game, and now I realize they were probably talking about the ZCross. I didn't even realize they might've been the ones who took the ZCross."

"This has been a huge help, really," Frank said. "Do you remember what they were wearing?"

Alana pulled a stool away from the counter and plopped down. "I think one had a gray T-shirt and the other was wearing a blue one. They both had on jeans."

Kevin shook his head. "No, no—you've got it all wrong. They were wearing sweatshirts. I'm sure of it."

Alana and Kevin started arguing. Joe wasn't quite sure what to write down, so he wrote down

Blue T-shirt & gray T-shirt OR two sweatshirts under the description of the suspects. This happened a lot. Most of the time witnesses couldn't remember what the suspects looked like, or they remembered different things.

"What about their hair color or their eye color?" Frank asked.

Alana let out a sigh. "I think they both had brown hair."

Kevin shook his head again. "One was blond, don't you remember?"

Frank glanced sideways at his brother. It was clear they weren't going to get Alana and Kevin to agree on anything. "If you remember anything else, let us know. We're going to look around the den one last time and see if we missed anything."

As they left, Alana and Kevin were still arguing. "Maybe he had red hair," Alana whispered, more confused than ever. "I just don't know anymore."

Joe and Frank shut the door to the den behind them. "So two boys took the ZCross," Joe said. "That makes sense. Now we just have to figure out which two boys. Do you think we should go through the photo booth pictures again?"

"They didn't give us a good enough description," Frank said, pacing the room. "Maybe there's more here . . . there has to be something we missed."

The boys started searching the room again, this time checking the cabinet beneath the television set and the small table by the couch. Sometimes when they returned to the scene of a mystery they found smaller clues they'd missed the first time. Frank knelt down and looked under the couch, while Joe examined the crumpled ZCross pamphlet again.

"Why would someone tear it apart?" Joe asked.

Frank was leaning over the back of the couch, reaching for something there. "Why would they tear the entire box apart?" he asked.

Joe thought it was a strange question until he realized what Frank had found. There, behind the couch, was the entire ZCross box. And one whole side of it was shredded. Joe stepped closer to get a better look. But it was empty.

"It's like someone ripped it. Do you think they

were trying to get it out of the box in a hurry?"

Frank opened the end, which was kind of slimy. "Ewww . . . it's wet. Gross."

He and Joe stood there, studying the shredded box. "Maybe they were trying to avoid being seen. The game box is smaller than a giant cardboard thing," Joe said. "Maybe they were hoping no one would notice them leave."

"Still," Frank said, "they didn't have to rip the box apart. This is so strange. It makes no sense."

Joe looked out the window at the party. Whoever did this had been here, as a guest. But why would they leave evidence behind? And what was the second boy holding, the one with the squirming stomach?

For the first time ever, the Hardy Boys were seriously stumped.

Chapter 8

FORGOTTEN EVIDENCE

"Let's see what we know so far," Joe said, plopping down on the couch next to his brother. He flipped open his notebook. "Who . . ."

Frank leaned over, looking at the page. Joe had crossed out the description Mr. Fun had given them of the girl with the purple shirt and pink streak in her hair. He'd crossed out the names Kendall and Lisi, too. Underneath he'd written:

Two boys

One held game under his shirt

One had squirming stomach

Blue T-shirt and gray T-shirt OR two sweatshirts

Both had brown hair (or maybe red?) or brown hair
and blond hair

Frank shook his head. "We don't really have much to work with," he said. "I guess we know that the boys aren't on the Bayport Bandits—otherwise they would have been wearing the same shirts we are. But besides that, these two kids could be anyone. What other clues do we have?"

Joe turned the page. "Just the other details about the ripped-up box. We're sure it's not Kendall and Lisi, right? Should we go back to them to see if they might have noticed the two boys Kevin and Alana saw?"

Before Frank could answer, there was a knock

on the den door. Kevin opened it and poked his head inside. "Um . . . I remembered one more thing!" he said, slipping in and shutting the door behind him.

Kevin sat down on a chair and started talking. "As the boys were leaving, I heard them say something about a guy named Mr. Fun. Do you think that was some kind of code?"

Joe laughed. "No, Mr. Fun is a real person. He's the owner of Fun World. You know, that arcade downtown?"

Kevin's eyes widened. "Ohhhh! Yeah, I used to go there all the time. I was obsessed with the Shooting Hoops game there."

Frank leaned in, listening closer. "Do you remember what they said about Mr. Fun?" he asked.

Kevin shook his head. Joe noticed that the front of his uniform shirt had a white smear on it. It looked like vanilla frosting. "No . . . just something about Mr. Fun. Then the one kid said, 'We could be back in half an hour.' They were going somewhere."

Joe scribbled down everything Kevin said, hoping it might be another lead. "Did they say where?"

"No," Kevin said. "They went into the garage, though. And then I didn't see them again. I still haven't seen them. But I'll tell you—I was right, one of the kids had blond hair, I swear. I don't know why Alana was arguing with me."

"Did they seem excited? Happy?" Frank asked. Maybe if they knew how the kids were acting, they'd be able to figure out why they'd taken the ZCross. It might have been that they really wanted it, just like everyone else. Or they might have had another reason.

Kevin took his glasses off and wiped them with his shirt. His eyes looked much smaller without them. "Now that you say that," he said, "they actually seemed kind of scared. Or maybe nervous? I could be wrong, but I remember thinking they didn't look like thieves."

Joe wrote down what Kevin said, including the detail about them looking scared or nervous. It was all just Kevin's opinion, not fact. Still, it was helpful to collect any information they could. "Do you remember anything else?" Joe asked.

Kevin shook his head. "I think that's it."

"We should check the garage," Joe said, turning to his brother. As Kevin went back into the kitchen, they headed there. When they got inside, through the side door, they didn't notice anything unusual. All Mr. Freeman's tools were on his workbench in the corner. Rakes, shovels, and brooms were hanging from hooks on the back wall. Mr. and Mrs. Freeman's cars weren't inside, just a few bikes the family had. Ellie's bike had a neon-pink stripe on the handlebars.

Frank looked around the garage, trying to find anything strange. "Whoever the kids were, I don't think they were interested in selling the ZCross."

Joe checked the rakes and brooms on the wall. "Why do you say that?"

"Because all of Mr. Freeman's tools are sitting right here. Power drills, electric saws . . . If they wanted to make money by selling things, wouldn't they have taken these, too?"

"Good point," Joe said, moving over to the bikes. "Bingo."

Frank turned around. "What is it? What did you find?"

Joe leaned over two of the bikes. They looked like they had just been taken out for a ride. They weren't leaning on the wall like the other two. Instead, they were in the middle of the garage and the kickstands were down. "Look right here," he said, pointing to one of the baskets.

Frank picked up the evidence to examine it. Inside a clear plastic bag were four tiny hot dogs. They were the same ones he and Joe had served the guests just a few hours before. "Do you think they took these as a snack?" Frank asked. He peered through the plastic bag at Joe.

"I don't know . . . maybe," Joe said. In the same basket was a black wallet. Joe opened it, hoping there would be clues

inside. There were a few worn baseball cards from some team called the Tigers. There was a smushed piece of bubble gum and three dollars. Joe flipped through the other compartments, hoping to find anything with a name on it, but there was nothing.

"There's not even a library card," Joe said, passing the wallet to Frank. "Nothing to tell us who it belongs to."

"Well, whoever took it, they'll come back for it," Frank said. "I doubt they'd just leave their wallet behind."

"What do you think about Mr. Fun?" Joe asked.

"I always liked Mr. Fun," Frank said, turning the wallet upside down. Two pennies fell out.

"Why would they mention him?" Joe asked. "Do you think it's just because he was the one who donated the prize?"

"Maybe," Frank said. "One thing's for certain, though. Whoever these boys are, they'll be back to get this wallet. We should be here when they do."

Joe scanned the garage. "A stakeout. That's a great idea. We'll need a place to hide, then."

The boys went to work, looking for the best spot they could find. They'd sit quietly, hidden somewhere close by, and watch. They'd wait as long as they had to. And when their two suspects returned, they'd be ready.

Chapter 9

THE MYSTERY MAN

Joe pushed back against the workbench, trying to get comfortable. He was wedged behind a stool, his knees against his chest. Whenever he tried to move, he got stuck. "I'm squished," he said.

Frank sat beside him, his arms wrapped around his knees. "Me too. Hopefully, it won't be much longer."

They'd been sitting under the workbench for a while. They'd pulled two stools in front of them so they'd be harder to see. Ten minutes in, Joe got hot. They had to open one of the giant garage doors to let some fresh air in.

At one point Mr. Freeman had come looking for them, and Frank and Joe had let him in on the plan. The dessert table was almost empty. People were still asking about what had happened, and Mr. Freeman worried that everyone would leave before they found the ZCross. The fund-raiser was almost over.

"Come on," Joe said, tapping his toe nervously. "Where are they?"

"They'll come," Frank said. "Just wait. We're so close, I can feel it."

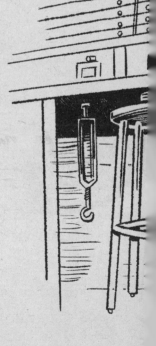

Joe watched the garage door, hoping one of the boys would appear outside. He leaned his head on Frank's shoulder. He was very sleepy. They'd spent the whole day getting ready for the party. With all the excitement of the case, Joe was ready for a nap. He tried to fight it, but he could feel himself falling asleep.

Suddenly Frank poked him in his side. "Pssssst!" he whispered. "Joe, wake up! Look!"

Joe rubbed his eyes. A boy was hovering by the

garage door. He had a blue baseball cap on, and the brim was pulled down so it was hard to see his eyes. Joe squinted, trying to make out his face, but the garage was dark and it was hard to see.

Sure enough, the boy went over to the bike. He took the wallet from the basket and slipped it into his back pocket. Then he took the plastic bag with hot dogs and threw it in the trash by the workbench.

When he turned back around, Frank and Joe saw their chance. They pushed out from under the workbench. "We need to talk to you," Frank said. "We have good reason to think you took the missing ZCross5000."

The boy's back was facing Frank and Joe. He straightened up when he heard Frank's voice. Then, without saying a word, he ran out of the garage and down the street.

"Get him!" Joe cried. He took off after the boy, Frank following close behind. They ran as fast as they could. Up ahead, the boy was running even faster. He turned the corner and sprinted up the block.

Joe tried to keep up. He cut through a neighbor's yard and watched as the boy disappeared into the woods behind Ellie's house. When Frank finally caught up to Joe, Joe stopped, his hands on his knees, trying to catch his breath.

"Where did he go?" Frank asked, looking into the trees. "Did we lose him?"

"I think so," Joe said. He could hear the boy running somewhere ahead of them, but he couldn't see him anymore. He wasn't even sure which direction he'd gone. He might have been headed back to Ellie's house, but he could have cut through the woods to the pond on the other side.

Just then Joe spotted something a few yards away. He ran over to it, picking up the cap the boy had left behind. He turned it over in his hands and looked inside. The tag had a name written on it. He brought it close to his face so he could read it.

"Of course," Joe finally said. "I should have realized it was him. The clues were there all along."

"What, what is it?" Frank asked. "What did you find?"

THE HARDY BOYS—and
YOU!

CAN YOU SOLVE THE MYSTERY OF THE VIDEO GAME BANDIT?

Grab a piece of paper and write your answers down.
Or just turn the page to find out!

1. Frank and Joe came up with a list of suspects.
   Can you think of more? List your suspects.

2. Write down the way you think the prized
   ZCross5000 disappeared.

3. Which clues helped you to solve this mystery? Write them down.

Chapter 10

A VERY NAUGHTY PUPPY

"It was Biff," Joe finally said. "But why?"

Joe handed his brother the blue cap. The tag inside read BIFF. Joe still had his name written on all his clothes from camp last summer. They made you do that so they could find them in the laundry.

"We should go find Phil," Frank said. "Come on, we can get back to the house through the woods. We just have to follow the music."

The boys took off through the trees. From

somewhere up ahead, they could hear the music from the party. The noise got louder and louder as they reached the back fence. They passed the tree house where they'd found Kendall. When they reached the edge of the woods, the party was just ending. A bunch of guests were grabbing their things and starting to leave.

"Thank you all for coming today," Coach Quinn said. "We've raised a lot of money for the Bayport Bandits, and we're nearly at our goal for the baseball trip fund."

Frank and Joe ran up to Phil, who was stationed by the sound system. They didn't want to accuse him of anything, but they knew that if Biff was the one who'd taken the ZCross, Phil had likely helped him. Kevin and Alana had agreed there were two boys coming out of the den, not one.

"Phil, we need to talk to you," Frank said. "We know Biff took the ZCross. We just need to know why. Does he still have it? What happened?"

Phil's cheeks turned pale. "Uh—oh no," he stuttered.

"It's okay, Phil," Joe said. "We just want to find it. We were hoping to have it auctioned off before everyone leaves. There's not much time."

Phil sighed. "I can explain, I swear," he said. "It was all a big misunderstanding. Right after the auction started, Biff and I went inside to check on Sherlock. And when we went into the den, we saw him with the ZCross5000. He had chewed half the box, and he was about to chew the remote, too!"

"We found the box," Frank said. "So I guess that was drool all over it? Yuck!"

Phil let out a small laugh. "Yeah, and when we saw it, we kind of freaked out. We knew it was the biggest prize of the auction, and Sherlock had destroyed the

box. That's when we remembered that Mr. Fun had gotten one for his birthday. We figured he might have the extra box at his house. We went there looking for it, but his son said they'd already thrown the box away."

"You could have told us," Joe said. "We would have understood."

"Well, we wanted to, but by the time we got back, everyone had already decided it was stolen. We panicked—we didn't know what to do." Phil put his face in his hands. "We should've said something . . . I realize that now."

"So the boy with the squirming stomach?" Frank said, looking at Joe. "Let me guess, did you or Biff put Sherlock under your shirt when you snuck out of the den?"

That made Phil smile. "Yeah . . . how'd you know?"

Frank didn't respond. Instead, he just laughed. "Well, maybe we can auction off the ZCross without the box. Do you still have it? Where is it?"

"Yeah," Phil said, waving for the boys to come

with him. "I think Biff was going to try to fix the old box. Come with me."

Frank and Joe followed Phil inside the house. Sure enough, when they got to the den, Biff was already there. His face was bright red, and he looked like he might cry. He had the ZCross in the package, but the box was still disgusting.

"It's no use!" he cried when he saw Phil. "It's totally messed up. We're going to get into so much—"

Before he could finish, he looked behind Phil and saw Frank and Joe there. "It's okay," Frank said. "Phil told us what happened. We're here to help. Let's talk to Coach Quinn. We might be able to auction off the ZCross even though it doesn't have the box. It's worth a try."

"We're so sorry we didn't tell anyone what happened," Phil said. "Really."

"Don't worry about it," Joe said, following Biff outside to the hall closet. He opened it. There, sitting behind some towels, was the chewed, soggy gaming system. Joe pulled it out, finally holding it in his hands. "Let's go—there's still time."

Ten minutes later Coach Quinn was back onstage. "Thank you for all your patience," she said. "We're very happy to say the ZCross5000 has been found, and it's ready for a new home! As some of you may have heard, we don't have a box for it. But I assure you it's in mint condition. The bidding starts at one hundred dollars."

Before she could even finish the sentence, three paddles in the audience went up. "Do I hear one hundred and twenty? One hundred and forty?" Coach Quinn asked. She kept raising the price, but even more paddles shot up. Everyone wanted the ZCross5000. It didn't matter whether it was in a box or not.

"This is unbelievable!" Joe exclaimed as the bidding reached three hundred dollars.

The boys watched as a woman with gray hair and an old man with glasses battled it out. Every time the woman raised her bidding paddle, the old man would raise his. After a few minutes the bidding war ended.

"Sold to the woman with the gray hair!" Coach Quinn said. Almost as soon as those words came out of her mouth, she froze. "I—I mean, sold to the woman in the blue scarf!" she stammered as everyone, including the woman, laughed. Coach Quinn laughed too. "I'm sorry, I didn't mean to be rude. I'm just so excited. That six hundred dollars will really help the Bayport Bandits get to their goal and to Florida. Thank you, everyone, and have a good night!"

The crowd clapped as the woman went up to get her prize, which Mrs. Freeman had put in a big, fancy silver gift bag. Frank put his arm around his brother, happy with how everything had turned out. They'd found the ZCross5000 and auctioned it off, and hopefully, the whole team would be going to Florida.

"We did it," Frank said, smiling. "Another case solved!"

Don't miss the next

HARDY BOYS
Clue Book:

#2 THE MISSING PLAYBOOK

As soon as their father pulled up to Cissy "Speedy" Zermeño's house, Joe Hardy threw open the car door and ran up to the house. Frank smiled and rolled his eyes at his eight-year-old younger brother. On the inside, though, Frank was just as excited as Joe was about the party at Speedy's. The annual Bandit Barbecue dinner meant the beginning of baseball season, his favorite time of year.

Frank grabbed the plate of brownies his mother

had made, and his parents followed him up the walkway to the Zermeños' front door. Joe had already disappeared somewhere inside, and Speedy was waiting at the door to greet them. Speedy's real name was Cissy, but she got her nickname from how quickly she did everything, from the speed of her legendary fastball to how quickly she talked.

"Hi-Mr.-and-Mrs.-Hardy-hey-Frank-come-on-in!" she said. *"I'm-so-excited-you're-here-wow-those-brownies-look-delicious!"*

"Hi, Speedy," Frank said. "How's the wrist?"

"Great!" Speedy held up her right hand. The last time Frank had seen her, a couple of days ago in school, she'd been wearing a brace. But now it was gone. *"The-doctor-said-the-sprain—"*

"Whoa, whoa!" Frank interrupted. "Slow down!"

Speedy laughed and took a deep breath before she spoke again, more slowly this time. "The doctor said my sprain is almost completely healed. He says I'll be able to pitch in our first game next week!"

"That's awesome!" Frank exclaimed. Speedy,

along with the rest of the team, had been worried when she'd hurt her wrist in gym class a couple of weeks ago. She was their star pitcher, and without her, they didn't stand a chance against their rivals the Jupiters.

"*Oh-I-know!* I can't wait to pitch the first game!" Speedy said.

Frank and Mr. and Mrs. Hardy followed Speedy outside to the backyard, where the barbecue was in full swing. Mr. and Mrs. Hardy stopped to talk to the other parents while Frank and Speedy went looking for Joe. They found him at the backyard swing set with the Mortons. Frank and Joe's best friend, Chet, was taking turns pushing his two younger sisters—Iola, who played for the Bandits, and Mimi, who went everywhere Iola did—on the swings. A camera was hanging from a strap around Chet's neck.

"Hi, Chet," Frank said. He nodded at the camera. "You taking pictures of the party?"

"Yup!" Chet said. He gave Iola a push and then grabbed his camera, holding it up for Frank to see.

"There are so many cool things you can do with this camera!" He began to explain to Frank how all the different buttons worked.

"Chet!" Mimi wailed. Her swing had come to a stop because Chet, distracted by his camera, had forgotten to push her. When Chet had a new hobby, he forgot about everything else.

"Oh, sorry," he said. He gave her a big push that sent her flying up into the air.

"What's that on your back, Mimi?" Joe asked.

"My new backpack!" Mimi said, kicking her feet to keep the swing going. "Isn't it cool? It's got butterflies on it!"

"She's starting preschool in the fall," Iola explained. "She's barely taken that backpack off since Mom bought it for her."

"Because it's *cool*!" Mimi said.

"Well, I'm starved," Iola said, hopping off her swing. "Who wants to get a hamburger?"

Everyone else said they were hungry too, except for Chet.

"But I'll come with you guys," he said. "I want to

take some pictures of the food. Coach Quinn said I could be the team's official photographer."

They all got into the line next to the grill. Speedy's dad was hard at work cooking up hamburgers and hot dogs, moving almost as fast as Speedy did. Standing in front of them in line was Tommy Dawson, who was an outfielder and relief pitcher for the Bandits, and Ezra Moore, who was new to the team.

"It's so unfair," Tommy complained to Ezra, loud enough that Frank could hear him. "I thought I was finally going to get to pitch."

"Sorry, dude," Ezra said, "but Speedy's the starting pitcher. You knew Coach Quinn was going to let her pitch as soon as her wrist was healed."

"She shouldn't be the starter anyway," Tommy said. "I'm ten times better than she is. Coach Quinn's just got it in for me. I'm not going to let her get away with this."

"Tommy, calm down," Ezra said.

"No way. Forget this stupid team!" Tommy snapped. He stalked off, ignoring Ezra's attempts to stop him.

Ezra noticed Frank listening in on their conversation.

"He'll cool off," Ezra said. "He's just disappointed."

Frank nodded. He was just glad Speedy hadn't heard what Tommy was saying.

The kids loaded up their plates with food and sat in the grass with some of the other Bandits to eat. When they were done, someone found a baseball and they started a game of catch. All the younger brothers and sisters of the Bandits players were sitting around Mimi, whose backpack was jammed full of coloring books, stuffed animals, and other toys that she was handing out. They played while the older kids tossed the ball and the parents watched, chatting as they sipped their cups of punch.

Soon it began to grow dark, and the party moved inside. The parents gathered in the kitchen while the little kids sat in front of the television in the living room to watch a movie. Mimi was among them, her empty backpack slung over her shoulders. While they watched the movie, most of the kids played with one of the toys or coloring books that Mimi had given them.

Meanwhile, Coach Quinn gathered all the Bandits together for a team meeting.

"Thanks for coming, everyone," she said when the team was sitting before her. "It's going to be the start of an awesome season, right?"

"Right!" they all replied. Joe's voice was the loudest of all, Frank noticed.

Coach Quinn's eyes twinkled. "That's what I thought. Now, let me show you our new secret weapon."

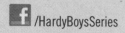

Nancy Drew
* CLUE BOOK *

Test your detective skills with Nancy and her best friends, Bess and George!

NancyDrew.com

Join Zeus and his friends as they set off on the adventure of a lifetime.

Now Available:

HEROES IN TRAINING

Uranus and the Bubbles of Trouble

Joan Holub & Suzanne Williams

#1 Zeus and the Thunderbolt of Doom

#2 Poseidon and the Sea of Fury

#3 Hades and the Helm of Darkness

#4 Hyperion and the Great Balls of Fire

#5 Typhon and the Winds of Destruction

#6 Apollo and the Battle of the Birds

#7 Ares and the Spear of Fear

#8 Cronus and the Threads of Dread

#9 Crius and the Night of Fright

#10 Hephaestus and the Island of Terror

Did you LOVE reading this book?

Visit the Whyville...

IN THE MIDDLE BOOK HIVE

Where you can:

- ⬡ Discover great books!
- ⬡ Meet new friends!
- ⬡ Read exclusive sneak peeks and more!

Log on to visit now!
bookhive.whyville.net